For Toby and Martha

First U.S. edition 2017

Library of Congress Catalog Card Number pending
ISBN 978-0-7636-9498-2

17 18 19 20 21 22 APS 10 9 8 7 6 5 4 3 2 1

Printed in Humen, Dongguan, China

This book was typeset in Plantin.
The illustrations were done in mixed media.

Candlewick Press
99 Dover Street
Somerville, Massachusetts 02144

visit us at www.candlewick.com

WILLY AND THE CLOUD

ANTHONY BROWNE

CANDLEWICK PRESS

It all began on a warm, sunny day when Willy decided to go to the park.
There wasn't a cloud in the sky when he set off.
(Well, just a little tiny one.)

That's a bit annoying, he thought.

The cloud seemed to be following him.

What's going on?

I think it's gone. . . .

Yes, it has gone. Phew!   (But Willy was wrong.)

At the park everyone seemed to be having great fun.

Willy just shivered.

So he went home.

Why was the cloud following him? What could he do?

"Hello," said Willy. "Is this the police?"

"Yes, sir. How can I help?"

"W-well, you see, I'm — I'm being followed."

"I see, sir. Who by? Can you give me a description?"

"Um . . . well, that's a bit difficult. It's — it's a cloud."

"You're being followed by a CLOUD, sir?"

"Yes — a BIG cloud . . ."

Willy heard the horrible sound of laughing policemen.

"Oh, dear," he said, and put down the phone.

This cloud is awful, thought Willy. *How can I get rid of it?*
The room was getting darker and darker, so he turned on
the light and closed the curtains.

After a couple of hours Willy nervously peered out the window. "Fantastic—it's gone!" he shouted.

(But he was wrong.)

Willy ran back inside. He felt miserable. The house was becoming very hot. He could hardly breathe. There seemed to be no air. He heard loud, rumbling noises outside, and slowly he began to feel angry. Eventually he could stand it no longer. He rushed outside. . . .

Everything went quiet. What was happening?
Was the cloud crying? It felt rather wonderful.
The soft, cool rain was delicious.
Willy felt like singing . . . and even dancing!

After a while the rain stopped and the sun came out.
I think I'll try the park again, thought Willy.

And this time when he got there,

EVERYONE was happy!